COPING WITH

a Hospital Stay

by Sharon Carter & Judy Monnig, R. N.

THE ROSEN PUBLISHING GROUP, INC./
NEW YORK

Published in 1987 by The Rosen Publishing Group, Inc.
29 East 21st Street, New York, NY 10010

First Edition

Library of Congress Cataloging-in-Publication Data

Carter, Sharon.
Coping with a hospital stay.

Includes index.
Summary: Offers tips to teenagers on handling a stay in the hospital, including checking in to the hospital, asking your doctor questions, coping with visitors, relieving boredom, and keeping up with school work.
1. Hospitals—Juvenile literature. [1. Hospitals]
I. Monnig, Judy. II. Title.
RA963.5.C37 1987 362.1'1 87-16634
ISBN 0-8239-0685-X

Manufactured in the United States of America

Contents

Chapter 1

Oh, No! Not. . .the Hospital!

The hospital? Me? You've got to be kidding! Uh. . .you *aren't* kidding.

Shots! Bedpans! Nurses! Uggghhhhhh.

Hospitals are for everybody, and a time may come when you have to stay in one, for any number of reasons.

It may not be fun, but it doesn't have to be terrible, either. Things are usually pretty much what you make of them, so if you plan on trying to do it in a hospital, too, you are almost sure to make things better.

A stay in a hospital can introduce you to other kids your age, and you may make good friends who share the same thing that is happening to you.

Or your stay in the hospital can help correct long-standing conditions, such as back problems or even heart problems.

Or maybe you didn't have a chance to plan anything. No one had any idea anything was going to happen, but suddenly there you are, flat on your back staring at the ceiling and wondering what in thunder hit you—even if you know all too well what hit you: somebody's 1980 Camaro.

People around you may not be a lot of help in coping with a hospital stay. Too often they trot out all the clichés: "Think how much worse off you could be!" "They're finding out new things about these diseases all the time!" "Just think, you don't have to go to school or anything. You can just lie around and get all this attention. Must be nice!"

A good part of how well you handle a hospital stay and what aftereffects it leaves with you concerns where you are in the hospital. More and more hospitals now have adolescent units, designed for people your age, where you can play rock and roll music, tack up a picture of Prince or Madonna, keep a cooler of soft drinks by your bed, and have fleets of friends in with nobody batting an eye.

Contrast that with gray walls, a mildew-green bedspread, and a great view of a brick wall; a nurse whose mouth looks sewed together in pinched disapproval; piped-in Lawrence Welk specials; and next door a geriatric screamer (an unfortunate fact of hospital life) who makes noises suggestive of a champion hog caller having a baby hippopotamus removed from his or her nose...need we go into further detail? Such an environment would depress a hyena, and when you've got a medical problem in addition, you really do have a situation difficult to cope with.

So first off, if you have *any* say in the matter, any advance notice, look over the hospital where you'll be a patient. Check out the adolescent facilities. Don't be hypercritical, because not every hospital is set up to handle people your age, but do try to find a good atmosphere if at all possible.

Of course, it may not be possible. You may have been admitted on an emergency basis. Or your doctor may not be on the staff of a hospital with better facilities. In that case you just have to bite the bullet and make the best of things.

But if you can, look over the hospital ahead of time. If nothing else, it helps you at least to get set for what is coming up. And it also impresses the staff that you are mature enough to look things over before you are admitted as a patient. A problem with a lot of younger patients is that they didn't want or plan to be in the hospital, they are angry at the world because it happened, and they take it out on everyone around them.

(Of course, a lot of hospital patients didn't want or plan to be there. If just happened. But older people may have a more balanced view: it was nobody's fault and they just have to put up with it.)

Ask what you will be permitted to bring. Hospitals differ a great deal in the matter of radios, blow dryers, hot rollers, video games, and so on. If you do have permission to bring such things from home, don't abuse the privilege. Nurses and doctors have been known to get fed up with a room ankle-deep in clutter and to order everything sent home.

A word of warning. If you are permitted to bring a radio or, more likely, have a radio in your room, *keep the volume low*! Probably the most common complaint teens hear these days is about radios at a volume that would register on the Richter scale. Typically, if your radio can be heard outside your room, you will be asked to turn it down. And if you don't turn it down, or if the request has to be repeated, expect it to be sent home or cut off to your room.

A hospital, after all, is full of sick people, and no one

is going to permit an inconsiderate lout to pound everyone else's head into the ground with noise just because that's the way the lout likes it.

Off the soapbox...in checking a hospital, talk to your doctor or to the head nurse. Ask what to expect. Don't be afraid of coming out with "dumb questions." (There really is no such thing as a dumb question. You ask because you don't know. If you don't know, the only way to find out is to get someone to tell you. So if in doubt, ask.) If you don't understand the answer—and medical people sometimes rattle off terms that sound like misspelled Russian to the rest of the world—ask for clarification.

What if whoever you are talking to *still* doesn't explain in terms you can understand?

That happens. Some people just can't seem to put things into plain and simple English. And some people are more interested in impressing us with their vast knowledge than they are in *communicating* with us.

So if you find yourself bumfuzzled about what is going to happen to you, don't stop until you get answers that you understand and that make sense.

If you run into a brick wall in this respect, ask to see the hospital chaplain or the patient representative. These people are there to help *you* deal with the nonmedical side of your stay and your hospital care.

Don't be afraid to do this, please! Being in a hospital can be unnerving for anyone, but if you have only a foggy idea of what is going on or what is to happen, it's ten times worse. The simplest procedure can be scary when you don't know why it is being done. You can be rolled down for what is actually a simple X-ray, but you personally don't know that and aren't sure if you are going to come out of that room as you or as the Bride of Frankenstein.

You have a right to know what is going on, what is being done, and why. The corny old soap-opera situation, "We aren't going to tell her 'the truth'—it would only upset her!" is actually illegal. A doctor who withholds the truth from an *adult* patient is laying himself or herself wide open for a malpractice suit.

Unfortunately, where you are concerned, that can be a problem. You probably aren't legally an adult yet. But if you want to know what is happening, it's a rare family or doctor who won't sit down and put it all in terms you can understand.

Chapter II

What to Ask Your Doctor

You need to be able to talk with your doctor. Talk, as in *communicate*. But that can be surprisingly difficult to do, as we indicated in the last chapter. So here are some questions that can make your stay easier to tolerate.

"Explain to me *exactly* what is wrong."

You have a right to know, and you have a right for it to be explained in terms you can understand. Don't be put off or intimidated into silence by, "You have a quadrilateral tear of the right medial malleolus..." Tell the doctor to cripple that and walk it by you slow—in other words, put it in five-cent, not five-dollar, terms.

"What is going to happen and am I going to get better and how long will that take?"

Maybe you had better break those up into separate questions. But do get the answers.

You do have a right to know. The silly soap opera situation, "Mary thinks she's going into the hospital for an ingrown toenail, but she really has terminal leprosy. We're not telling her because it would just upset her and wouldn't do any good," is not only dumb, it's illegal. The patient has the right to know his condition; the doctor has the responsibility to tell him.

But what if the patient is a minor? We asked a number of both doctors and lawyers that question and got such a wide variety of answers that we concluded there are no real guidelines. When you are under eighteen, all the rules are different.

But we did not find any doctors who said they would choose to lie to a youngster about his or her condition unless the parents absolutely ordered it; and most doctors said they would not lie even then.

"Face it, we usually have a pretty good idea what is going on with our own bodies," one surgeon said. "We usually know, even if just on an instinctual level, when something isn't working right. I wouldn't lie to patients, even young patients. Because sooner or later they are going to know the truth, and how could they trust anything I did after that?"

Very good points.

"What can I expect here in the hospital? What will treatment be like? How will I feel? Will it hurt? Will medication make me sick?"

Something that is explained ahead of time, even if it's unpleasant, is almost always easier to handle. Some people don't agree with that, saying that if you are dreading it you get more tense and nervous and anxious. But as a general rule, knowing what is coming makes it easier to handle.

"What can I do here? Can I have a radio? When can friends visit me? What about school? Can I do things like put up posters?"

Those questions may seem too small and silly to "bother" a doctor with, but they aren't. For however long, that hospital room is going to be your world, and we personally think you should be able to make it feel as much like home as possible. We think you should be able to put up a few posters, play Madonna or The Boss as long as you don't disturb anyone else, have plants, have friends in, bring a bedspread from home.

"Maybe I don't want to talk about what's wrong with everyone who comes in. What should I tell them?"

You have a right to keep your medical problems private. Once again, that is not a silly question, and it's one your doctor is likely to have dealt with before. Don't be shy about asking, because your doctor is very likely to have some good responses.

"What things do I need to tell you about—like odd pains or something like that?"

That may sound dumb, but it really isn't. You may not think to tell the doctor, when he or she visits, about the odd pulling sensation around the incision, but it could be something your physician needs to know. Discussing ahead of time what you should be alert for helps both you and your doctor. Moreover, it really helps to open up communication lines between you.

"What can I do to help me get better?"

Of everything you ask, this will probably make your doctor the happiest.

What if you have a doctor you just can't talk to? He stares down his nose as if you were a subhuman species, mutters a few indistinct phrases, and hurries off, leaving you uneasy and bewildered.

First, consider that you may be partly at fault. Do you give the impression you are someone an adult can communicate with? We aren't joking here. If you have a long, dangling earring—and you're a guy—blue hair, and a punk getup that wasn't whipped with an ugly stick—the whole tree fell on it—you certainly know that most adults don't find it easy to communicate with you. (That may be the whole point!)

There are times and places to gross out the old folks and establish *your* place in time and the world, and there are times and places to cool it. Now is a time to cool it. Tone it down.

Your doctor may be an "I'm too busy to bother" type, which is infuriating to most patients. If the doctor will take your money and take charge of your life but is too busy to bother answering your questions, we'd say shop for another doctor!

Your doctor may just be a jerk. The profession is no more immune to this affliction than any other field. Again, if possible, try to find another doctor.

In the meantime, ask a resident or medical student, if one is around. Or a nurse. He or she may not be able to answer all your questions without clearance from the doctor, but keep after it.

It's your body and your life. You have a right to know.

If you are facing surgery, ask about the risks—and *any* surgery has risks. Get the answers in plain English, not in terms three miles above your head.

You need to know approximately how long you will be in the hospital and when you can return to school and to normal living, for example, taking part in sports.

Ask what kind of medicine you will be getting and what it is for. Ask very specific questions about what the medicines are expected to do and what side effects they might have. What is considered an overdose, and how will it make you feel?

You need to know how much pain you can reasonably expect and how to deal with it. If you will be taking pain medicine, be sure to understand the instructions on how to take it when you leave the hospital.

Ask about the possibility of addiction. We aren't kidding! In all the current uproar over teens and drugs, we never hear that some kids have become hooked through pain medications prescribed by their doctors, but believe us, it certainly happens! And it has been fatal!

(Statistics lately seem to show that teens—if perhaps not always their elders—are beginning to learn the lessons taught by a string of drug deaths, from Janis Joplin to Len Bias. When more kids are deciding that dope really is for dopes, you don't want to develop a problem due to a *prescription*, for cats' sake!)

Ask about alternatives to help control pain, such as hot showers or exercises. It may sound dumb, but those things can really help.

If you will be needing special equipment at home, such as a wheelchair or crutches or exercise equipment, find out and make arrangements for it ahead of time instead of waiting until you are leaving the hospital. That can turn into a complicated and nerve-wracking mess for everyone.

Then remember that each patient and each illness can be different, and what the doctor tells you should be used as *guidelines*. If you don't react the way the doctor said, it doesn't mean that he or she was telling you wrong; no case is strictly "by the book."

Chapter III

Coping with Visitors You Wish Would Stay Home

Usually, when you are stuck in a hospital, visitors are the highlight of the day—cheering you up, bringing you news of the "outside world," making you feel more in touch with what's going on and less like you've been exiled to Outer Mongolia, and demonstrating that people care enough about you to take time to drop by.

Usually, we said. Not always.

Because there are those people who seem to materialize like ectoplasm at the first hint of bad news. Five minutes of them makes the morgue seem cheerful by comparison.

You know the type. They tend to be elderly female relatives who rarely wear anything but black, gray, and the sort of purple that makes you feel weepy just looking at it.

A typical visit goes like this. They surge through the door already on the verge of tears, handkerchief in hand. If you are lucky you have something in plaster and they can't hug you. They next wail, "Oh, you poor little ba-beee!" the last a rising banshee wail. (Don't you *love* it?) "What a horrible thing to happen to you!" They go on and on and *on* about what's wrong with you and unblushingly ask the most personal questions, usually in tones that can be heard on the next floor—upstairs *and* down.

After they have exhausted you as a topic of conversation, they go into everything sad that has happened to anyone they know.

Then it's everyone they ever heard of who had what you have and died of it.

If you aren't likely to croak from whatever is wrong, they will tell you of scores of people—"fine young people just like you"—who went to the hospital to have a hangnail taken care of, got the wrong medication, and became a vegetable. Get the picture? These people give every cloud a pitch-black lining.

We all know people like that. They are surprisingly common even though the world in general holds them in low esteem (and occasionally by the neck and under water.)

Other types who make your hospital stay grim can be harder to spot. They may not actually say anything you could object to, but they nevertheless manage to leave you with feelings you don't like.

Adults may do it, and your friends may be the culprits (sometimes unwitting ones) as well.

For example, a classmate is visiting. He spends the whole time standing up, which puts you at a disadvantage because you have to crane your neck uncomfortably to talk. He holds his arms folded across his chest and rocks back on his heels now and then. He doesn't say anything wrong—but you feel gloated over, as if he thinks you deserve what happened and he's not the least bit sorry.

Other people want to know the details of your medical problems, and they ask personal questions that are none of their business.

Still other people, usually relatives that you haven't seen in years, now feel duty bound to come and sit by your bed and natter endlessly about such fascinating things as family squabbles that happened ten years before you were born. The only thing less interesting you can think of would be a postgraduate lecture on the social structure of an ant colony.

There are people who point out "for your own good!" how you are responsible for what happened and if you hadn't wanted to play football "and had listened to your mother because she didn't want you to play either!" you would not now be there with a broken leg; or if you had taken care of yourself "and not eaten all that junk food and run around all the time, you wouldn't have come down with ___________" You fill in the blank. Whatever you have or whatever happened, they can find a way to wag a moral finger at you.

There are the people who just plain bore you to the screaming point! They are usually bionic mouths who could outtalk a congressional filibuster with one tonsil tied behind them, usually on a subject in which you couldn't possibly have less interest. You try to be polite, prop an eyelid open, and think they'll come in handy if surgery ever runs out of anesthesia.

And the people who believe in being "totally honest"—total honesty being, "Boy! Do you look terrible. I'll bet that hurts; it sure looks awful. Are you going to have a scar?"

There are people who say the most cutting things,

and if you aren't amused they look hurt and say, "Hey, I was just *teasing*! Can't you take a joke?" thereby having made you look bad on two counts. (In or out of the hospital, in any situation, jerks like this are the kind of pain in the anatomy well deserving of a nasty accident themselves.)

When you are well, all these people tend to be half funny and half irritating, but at least you are mobile and can get away from them. When you are flat on your back with an IV in your arm, you are stuck.

Or are you?

The answer is no, and let's consider why you shouldn't be.

When you are well, especially if you know what these people are like, you can and probably do let such things roll right off—or go several city blocks to avoid them. But in a hospital, when you are sick or have been hurt, you are a lot more vulnerable.

Dr. Norman Neaves, senior minister of the Church of the Servant (United Methodist), Oklahoma City, has some suggestions for dealing with Griselda Gloom, Fork-tongued Freddy, and their assorted ilk.

"First, be every bit as aware of your own feelings as you are what has been said. Be aware of the effect of words. It's okay to feel, or even say, 'Hey, I don't like that! That doesn't make me feel very good!'

"And the downer message may not be in the words, but in the way they're said. People can say, 'Well, you don't look like you feel all that bad' and make it sound sarcastic, like they think you are faking. They can say it as a flat statement of fact. Or they can say it like it's congratulations, that it's great you don't feel that bad.

"Trust your feelings about something like that. If

something strikes you as a put-down, even though the actual words themselves didn't say that, your feelings are probably right on target about what was *meant*. Your feelings are there to guide you. Let them."

Dr. Neaves suggests that you parry unwelcome comments with humor, if possible, or at least with good nature. "If someone says you look terrible, say, 'What do you expect? I'm in the hospital! May I congratulate you on your keen sense of the obvious?'"

Friends your own age can sometimes be clumsy or hurtful in what they say simply because the situation is new to them and they don't know how to handle it. They may kid and joke, sometimes hurtfully, to keep their own feelings under control.

If that happens, just change the subject. Ask about school, or basketball, or what other friends are doing.

"Try, too, to learn to form an inner shield against the effect of negative input," Dr. Neaves suggests. "It takes a mental effort to say to yourself that you aren't going to let so-and-so's tactlessness get through and bother you, but you can do it.

"Talk to your parents about people who really do bug you. If they say, 'Oh, that's just her way. She doesn't mean anything by it, and saying anything would hurt her feelings,' remind them that this person is also hurting *your* feelings, and right now you are the one with the problem.

"And talk to the doctor and the nurses. You *do* have the power to request that certain people not be allowed to visit. Moreover, you have the right. A mental downer or being upset never helped anyone overcome a physical illness or injury.

"If you are depressed and down, if things or people

really are getting on your nerves and you need to talk to someone, ask to speak to a hospital chaplain. A lot of people don't do that because they're afraid the chaplain will come charging through the door and start right in on religion.

"That's not so. Any chaplain who did would be replaced. The chaplain is there to discuss your feelings, to help you with your problems. So do ask a nurse or doctor to send the chaplain to see you. You will almost surely be glad you did."

One type of visitor that is hard for anyone to deal with, but especially hard for people your age, is Little Mary Sunshine. You may be in pain, have a life-threatening illness, have serious burns, and this person is so determinedly cheerful she's nauseating. If you were spouting arterial blood she'd probably chirp that it was a nice healthy red! If you say you feel down and hate the whole total universe, LMS twitters, "Oh, no, you don't *really* hate anyone! We are just a bit grumpy this morning, aren't we? But it will soon pass."

People like that are more than maddening. They are confusing, especially to young people. We feel that we *should* like those who are bright and cheerful and trying to make us happy. We should—but more often we'd like to throttle them. These people are really saying, "I don't care what your feelings are. Don't do or say or admit anything sad because that would depress *me* and that's not allowed!"

"Again, trust your feelings," Dr. Neaves says. "Don't think 'What's wrong with me?' if this 'nice, sweet' person makes you want to throw a pillow at her. It's enough that he or she does. This person, also, you can request not be allowed to visit anymore.

"You have the right to guide the conversation and the tone of visits. Don't abuse that power, but do use it. Right now you have been hurt or are sick, and while you get better you are in the driver's seat."

Chapter IV

Getting Along with a Roommate

Sharing a hospital room with another patient is something of a Catch-22.

It can get awfully lonely all by yourself. On the other hand, a roommate, especially in such close and intimate quarters, can drive you absolutely stark ravers.

There is one thing to be said for large hospitals: They usually have adolescent units and you are likely to have a roommate of about your age and—hopefully—interests. But it can be sheer misery on top of the misery that landed you there in the first place to have to share territory with a senior citizen who complains (generally nonstop) that rock music, video, and any hair style but the one he or she wore at your age mean that you are doomed to spend eternity slowly roasting on a pitchfork. (I have talked to teens to whom exactly that has happened. One boy said, "I told the nurse one night if she didn't move me or him, I was walking out—and I'd broken both legs in a car wreck!")

But even having a roommate about your age is no guarantee that things will go well. Some actual complaints of teens we talked with:

"She had a voice that sounded like it was coming from a stable—I mean, I love horses but a whinny isn't a particularly pretty sound, right? I had just broken up with my boyfriend and was sad about that, and she talked twenty-six hours a day about hers. I mean, you talk about the Bionic Mouth! On top of everything else, after her going on and on about how wonderful and handsome and great he is, he comes in and the guy's a geek! We're talking world class geek! By the end of four days I was thinking at nights of getting up and putting a pillow over her head!"

"The guy was a year older than I, but the biggest *baby* in the world! He'd broken a leg water skiing, and he whined and moaned and cried and felt sorry for himself. And his mother came in two or three times a day and whined and cried and moaned about 'her baby.' Her baby, all right! He should have been in diapers!

"I'd been really hurt. I mean, I was in a motorcycle accident and I lost a kidney and a lot of other things were messed up, and he always had a big herd of relatives in every evening, bumping into my bed and throwing coats and purses on it like I wasn't even there! I don't think any of them ever said more than 'Hi' to me. They all sniveled and whined over the jerk with the leg broken in one place! I finally said move me or I'm going to give him something to cry and whine *about*! Like a mouth with no teeth in it."

We could go on and on, but you get the picture.

What if you do have or will have a roommate? Here are some ground rules for getting along.

Say, right from the start, "Can we establish a few guidelines here? I like rock and roll and can't stand country and western music. I like TV mysteries and can't stand game shows. What about you?" You've at least opened the way for an agreement on what you will watch and listen to. It's far better to do that than to endure his or her tastes and then blow sky high about them—which is too often the way it happens.

Remember that a hospital patient is *not* responsible for his or her visitors and shouldn't be answerable for what they do—up to a point. The boy with the blubbering baby in the next bed should have said something right from the start about the rudeness of his visitors, although people as self-centered and insensitive as this group of clods seemed to be generally give you a blank look and then do exactly what they've been doing all along. They never think you mean *them*.

Speak up about things that bug you *before* you reach the explosion stage. (That's a good rule for any situation, by the way. Too many of us hold things in until we can't do it any longer and then blow up—when the other person had no idea how we felt or that something was really bothering us.)

If you are to go home tomorrow, something that your roommate is doing that sets your teeth on edge probably isn't worth making a fuss over. But if you are going to be there for a while, talk to your doctor, a nurse, or the chaplain about the problem.

We don't particularly recommend that you talk to parents, at least in most cases. All too often we hear, "Don't ask them to move you; that would hurt his (her) feelings too much! Don't let a little thing like that bother you; just concentrate on getting well." Parents are way too good at that. They're saying, in effect, "Your roommate's feelings count; yours don't." Well, you are the one who is sick or hurt; you are the one lying there staring at the ceiling and spending twenty-four hours a day two or three feet from someone whom you are beginning to fantasize about burying in an ant hill.

True, when we are sick or hurt we are more irritable and edgy and just plain cantankerous than we would normally be, but that's part of problems that land you in the hospital, and there's not one blessed thing you can do about it.

Be willing to say, "I just broke up with my boyfriend, and it really makes me sad to hear you talk so much about yours. Could we go on to other things?" Or "I don't really feel like talking very much, and it seems rude just to lie here and not say anything back to you. Besides, I have a headache. Do you have a book you could read for a while or something?" People often chatter out of nervousness, and asking them to be quiet may be all you need to do.

Sometimes nobody is really at fault when you can't get along or be happy with a roommate. A fairly quiet person may enjoy a chatty roommate because he or she doesn't have to carry the conversational ball, or may be driven batty by the sound of a verbal marathon.

And when something is really bothering you, irritating you, putting you on edge, and making you tense, it *isn't* going to help the process of your getting well.

So tell somebody you want to be moved. Don't abuse the privilege, but do remember that in the hospital you should be the one in control as much as possible.

Chapter V

If You Have a Choice of Hospitals

When you are considering hospitalization, you may not have a choice of which hospital to use, for a variety of reasons. Only one hospital in your area may specialize in what you need. Or your doctor may not be on the staff where you'd really like to go. Or in an emergency, you may end up at the nearest emergency room.

Or your doctor may only practice in one hospital, or may particularly recommend a certain hospital because of specialized equipment or nursing care, or any number of reasons. Be sure he spells out those reasons for you if he (or she) has strong feelings about one hospital over another. You have the right and the need to know.

Hospitals are just like any other institution, such as schools. They earn reputations in their community that are sometimes good and sometimes bad. Before you take someone else's word on the merits of a hospital, check it out for yourself.

Visit the hospital before you are scheduled to be admitted. Are the people in the Business Office nice and easy to talk with? Go up to a patient-care floor, preferably the one where you will be. Walk around the nurses' station and general area there, and try to get a feel for the staff's attitude toward both patients and visitors.

Find out if all the things needed for your care are available at that hospital or whether you will have to go to another one for specialized treatment or diagnosis. For example, a certain type of X-ray machine may not be available where you are scheduled to be admitted.

Probably no hospital exists in the world that doesn't have someone who'll tell you of bad experiences there. (A good friend had very bad experiences, not once but *twice*, at one of the most famous hospitals in the United States. She shudders if you mention the name and says she'd rather go to a good veterinarian than back there!)

But keep this in mind when you listen to other people's opinions of a hospital.

People in hospitals are rarely at their best, either the patients or their families. It is a stressful time, and they are usually very intolerant, which means that any small or large situation can easily be blown out of proportion.

For instance, a late meal can become a source of irritation that can be compounded by a nurse who doesn't have time to talk to patient and family as long as they would like.

So the complaint can build from terrible food (which is unfortunately more often true than not, according to the R.N. half of this team) to poor nursing care (which all too often comes from being under staffed, with not enough time to spend with each patient). Before long "everything" about this hospital is just awful!

Keep an open mind and an appreciation of everyone's troubles, and it will help contribute to a good hospital stay for all concerned.

Chapter VI

Don't Be a Patient the Nurses Want to Kick

As mentioned before, your nurses will take care of you whatever their personal feelings about you. But it's a lot easier to properly and cheerfully help someone who is at least making an effort to cooperate.

As we have also mentioned previously, someone down with a serious illness or having had a bad accident is very likely to lash out at the nearest moving targets and take out anger on family, friends—and nursing staff.

Most of the medical personal you come in contact with understand that and make allowances for it. But nobody, and that includes you, is willing to be a whipping post for too long.

If you have never been in a hospital before, you may not be aware of what the nurse's job involves. It is much more than passing out pills or giving shots. It involves changing dressings, emptying bedpans, changing bed linens with the patient still in bed, observing patients for developing problems and notifying doctors before the problems become major or life-threatening, listening to patients, and listening to families.

Basically, it comes down to having too many things

to do and not nearly enough time to do them all, or not enough staff to do everything when it needs to be done or as soon as the patient or his or her family thinks it should be done.

You can do some things that will help in your everyday care. First, in most hosptals, the best staffed shift is the 7 a.m. to 3 p.m. shift. That is the time of day when most of the routine physical care of patients is done, such as bathing, changing beds, serving two meals, and feeding patients who cannot feed themselves.

The evening and night shifts are staffed with fewer people, since the routine patient care diminishes as the day winds down.

Now it can be a problem for a patient who doesn't want the bath in the daytime to change his or her habits, but it is a bigger problem for the nursing staff when a patient decides he or she wants a bath and a shampoo at supper time or just before bedtime when there is just enough staff at work to manage nighttime medicines and treatments. To have to devote an hour or more to one patient can hopelessly snarl a nurse's schedule so that for the rest of that shift *everything* runs late.

So cooperate with schedules, and don't insist on doing it *your* way.

Another thing to remember is that your nurse isn't exclusively *your* nurse. She or he has other patients, sometimes as many as ten or twelve. When you ask for something, the nurse can rarely walk through the door with whatever you want as soon as you are through speaking. As in the emergency room, patient care is *not* on a first-come-first-served or first-requested-first-delivered basis. The nurses' and doctors' first response is going to be to the most urgent problem, working down to the least urgent. If you want a drink of water, the nurse is going to respond first to the patient who has pulled out an IV.

So be patient. However, if the wait really does get too long, call again. Messages are not always relayed. And if there has been a life-threatening emergency—say a patient has had a heart attack (cardiac arrest is the correct term, and if you hear the PA call "Code Blue," that is what has happened)—your request may have been totally forgotten in trying to save the patient's life.

When you want something, think a minute before you press the call button. Is there anything else you are likely to want or need any time soon? A Coke, or juice? A pen or pencil? If so, ask for everything at once. If you ask for four things, one right after the other, you make the nurse run up and down the hall four times when one trip would have been enough. Patients who do that aren't near the top of anyone's favorite-patient list.

Nursing is a hard, demanding, responsible job. (Notice how tired most nurses look by the end of their shifts.) The biggest single thing you can contribute to helping the medical staff care for you is the liberal use of common courtesy. It makes for mutual respect and cooperation.

Chapter VII

How to Keep from Getting Bored Cross-eyed

One of the biggest problems for most patients, even in a short hospital stay, is acute boredom. And the more immobilized you are, the more bored you are almost sure to be. People have brushed off boredom in the past as minor, something you can live with. But recently it has begun to come to light that boredom is one of the most stressful things that can happen to a human.

A friend of one of the authors is Dr. Jay Shirley, an internationally known research psychiatrist whose studies in the Antarctic provided a basis for a lot of the psychological background of the space program.

According to Dr. Shirley, "Boredom is terribly stressful! Boredom is the basis for a great deal of emotional trouble and even a lot of criminal behavior. Don't *ever* underestimate the problems it can cause you, including making physical problems worse or even leading to psychosomatic illnesses."

Okay, boredom is real and all that. How do you cope with it?

One of the best ways is to set yourself a challenge of some kind.

You might decide to learn a new skill, or to learn as

much about a subject as possible. That will almost certainly require the cooperation of a friend or relative, because hospital libraries tend to run heavily to Western and improbable romance novels.

One fifteen-year-old, in the hospital with a leg broken in five places in a car accident, had decided he wanted to be a pilot after seeing *Top Gun* three times. As he was about to come totally unhinged from boredom, his uncle (a pilot) suggested that he study for the written examination required for a pilot's license. The uncle brought him all the materials and coached him when necessary. When he had that down, the uncle brought him a steady stream of books about flying, ranging from the classic *Wind, Sand and Stars*, to how-tos on flying, to the best-seller *Yeager.* When the young man got out of the hospital, the uncle found a flight instructor who signed off permission for him to take the written test. He made a 98 on it and is now sacking groceries to pay for flying lessons. The grinding boredom of a long hospital stay is something he barely remembers in the excitement of what he gained by turning the enforced immobility to his advantage.

LuAnn was fourteen when her doctor made the shattering discovery that she had cancer. She underwent surgery and began chemotherapy, which had the usual side effects such as making her hair fall out.

But LuAnn was determined to make all this work to her advantage, since life had handed her such a cruel blow as cancer. She had always been chubby, and she asked the help of her doctor and the hospital dietitian to get some pounds off. Then she read every "how to be beautiful" book she could get her hands on. (Some were silly, some outrageous, and some had really good advice.) In her hospital bed she began experimenting with makeup. The nurses, who admired her spirit and courage, helped and offered advice and ideas, as well as honest evaluations of the results of her efforts.

When LuAnn went home, a secretary who had been a home economics teacher volunteered to visit her one or two nights a week and teach her to sew and make the clothes to go with her new image. (LuAnn's family didn't have a lot of money, and her hospitalization, even with insurance, had been hard on them financially.)

Today LuAnn is sixteen. The cancer has shown no signs of recurring, and she was recently a Homecoming Princess at her school. During her stay in the hospital, LuAnn learned that beauty is as much illusion as reality and that she could create the illusion well enough to overcome the rather ordinary looks she really did have.

If you have always wanted to try your hand at writing stories, a hospital stay is the time to do it. Granted, you may not have, or be able to use, a typewriter, and writing longhand is a chore. But what else do you have to do? Right now, probably nothing.

If you have never been much of a reader, a hospital stay tends to be more difficult. Watching TV and listening to the radio get old fast. You might try picking up the reading habit—it will be a lifelong asset.

Is there a subject that really interests you? Football? Rock music? Getting into television as a newsman or newswoman? How to do well in the business world? Chances are, if someone will go to the public library, they can bring you more books on the subject than you can read in a month.

You probably wouldn't want to spend all your time reading; even that gets tiring after a while. Games also make a good diversion. Ask friends or family to bring them and to come prepared to play you in Trivial Pursuit or chess or whatever. Games provide a challenge and interaction with other people that help make the time weigh less heavily on your hands.

Crafts projects are also good, but be sure they are something you really want to do. Such projects can be a nuisance if well-meaning visitors bring them as gifts; you feel guilty if you don't do anything with them, and you become irritable and edgy if you work on them because you feel you *have* to or you'll hurt Uncle Mortimer's feelings. One of the best defenses against that sort of gift is to start something—building a model or knitting a sweater—early in the game and then explain to Uncle Mortimer that you'll get to the plastic-flower kit as soon as you finish what you are working on.

Do make plans right from the start to cope with boredom. Don't underestimate or let anyone else underestimate the harmful effects boredom can have on you. Even a hospitalization of a few days, if you aren't prepared for its insidious effects, can produce painful, grinding, *harmful* boredom.

Chapter VIII

Keeping Up with Your Schoolwork

If your stay in the hospital is to last very long, you will need to keep up with your schoolwork while you are there. Falling behind and then having to catch up is a drag, and it can and almost certainly will make your whole situation much more difficult.

If you are scheduling your hospitalization, you may be able to arrange homework ahead of time with your teachers, and a tutor may not be necessary.

But if you didn't schedule this trip, or you are finding it difficult to keep up with what teachers want, a tutor can be very helpful. If so, talk with your doctor and nurses to find the best time to schedule this person to come in and help you with your studying.

You will need to set aside a certain amount of time for the tutor to work with you without interruptions. Ask the nurses to put a No Visitors sign on your door, and you might put the telephone off the hook. Then pitch in and get busy studying.

Following this regime will also help to keep you on a schedule and give you a sense of accomplishment, making you feel that your particular world isn't going off and leaving you. That can do a lot to help you fight depression.

If medication you are taking or a physical problem such as a broken arm or hand prevent you from writing, you might be able to make arrangements with your teachers for some other means of doing assignments, such as tape recordings.

The hospital itself may be able to help you. Some hospitals now have tutoring programs to be sure young patients do not fall behind in their schoolwork.

Keeping up is important for more reasons than just that it is what you are "supposed" to do. Hospitalization is hard on young people; to get behind in school and have to face the multiple problems of physical recovery, getting back into the social swing, *and* trying to dig out from under a mountain of schoolwork can be so depressing that it hurts every aspect of their recovery—physical, mental, and emotional.

Chapter IX

When You are Admitted from the Emergency Room

Going into a hospital as a patient isn't fun under any circumstances—at least that we can think of. But being admitting on an emergency basis is especially traumatic. One minute you were all right, the world looked good, things were going swell—then, wham! You broke your leg playing football. Or that funny pain in your side was suddenly burning like a white-hot fire. Or you vaguely remember seeing the grill of the other car coming at you. Or you don't remember seeing the grill of the other car coming at you. Or you don't remember the explosion and the fire, but looking at your burned arms and legs you know they happened. . .and suddenly your life was blown to hell.

For most of human history men (and to a lesser extent women) were supposed not to be affected by things like that. We were supposed to "take it like a man," "Hey, look, it's over. Forget it!" "That happened a *month* ago! Will you stop talking about it and get on with your life?" But more recently psychologists and psychiatrists have come to find that heavy trauma —whether we are victim, witness, or a relative of a victim—can tear our life to shreds. Because the trauma is under the surface and unseen, frequently unsuspected, it can cause us all kinds of disabling emotional and even physical problems.

So here is what to expect if an emergency, an illness or an accident, yanks the rug out from under you and lands you in the hospital.

Expect to feel anger and a sense of being betrayed. Your fury may have a target: the driver of the car that hit you, the guy whose illegal clip snapped a bone. Or you may not be able to pinpoint a culprit: Your bicycle blew a tire as you were going downhill fast. There's no one guilty party, but all the same you feel a boiling rage at *something* for messing up your life like this.

The problem with that kind of rage is that it tends to boil over on everything in its path. Psychologists call it "displacement." It is what happens when we don't have a specific target for our anger, or we are afraid to direct the anger where it rightly belongs.

For example, a factory worker has a run-in with his boss. He needs the job, so he can't tell the boss where to head in and what he thinks of him into the bargain. He'd get fired. So he goes home and beats his wife or slaps his kid across the room. He has taken out his anger on a target he knows is not a threat.

All of us do that, to some degree. In a way, it's a mechanism we use to protect ourselves from getting our teeth knocked out or our heads smashed. But it doesn't make life very pleasant for our emotional lightning rod, the person we picked to snarl at or abuse.

Here, once again, is a good place to ask to see the hospital chaplain. Tell him or her how you feel and that you have developed this overwhelming urge to snarl, growl, and snap. Maybe you already have started doing so. Your mother's worried sick about you anyway, and the last two times she's come to visit you've had her in tears, you've been so hateful and rude. And you feel bad about it, but you can't seem to stop.

The chaplain, believe me, will not only understand but admire you for facing up to this painful and destructive situation. (Some kids in the hospital, because they know they can get away with it, ride it for all it is worth—and they ought to be spanked for it!)

There are various ways of dealing with your anger, once you realize that it is normal and to be expected. Just don't let it become destructive, or it will make a bad situation far worse.

Fear is another feeling common to an emergency hospitalization. Fear and a feeling that life has betrayed you. This wasn't supposed to happen! It wasn't supposed to be like this! If life can do *this* to me, what else awful is likely to happen? Your confidence, your feeling that you can do anything at all may totally desert you. The thought of going back out into the world is terrifying!

Depression is common here as well. It comes from a feeling of loss of control and of helplessness. You may wake up and have a couple of bites of breakfast, then stare at the ceiling and be vaguely aware an aide is taking away the tray—and suddenly you realize they are bringing *lunch*. The entire morning passed with you staring at the ceiling, your mind a gray blank.

It may not be that bad, or it may be worse. The thing is, it's normal; expect it and be prepared to deal with it.

You may feel guilty about whatever happened even though, by all logic, not one thing you could have done would have made a bit of difference.

Or some of that guilt may be roosting right where it

belongs: You *were* driving too fast. You *had* had a couple of beers.

Guilt is one of the most corrosive emotions of the human race, and one of the least useful. It can make us totally miserable but do nothing whatever to reshape our behavior in a constructive way. It makes us miserable but gives us nothing to improve our lives.

Some parents work at piling on the guilt. They have the idea that if they make their kids feel guilty about everything wrong, that miserable feeling will make the kids act like angels. And that's not true. All guilt does is warp you inside.

If you have these feelings, or others that are making you unhappy, talk to someone about them. They may be normal, but they can also twist you up inside at a time when your mind and body have enough to do just getting you well. Let's not concentrate on making things worse!

Does it sound like a cop-out (do you still use that term?) our telling you to talk to someone on the counseling or chaplain staff? We hope not. We don't think a book that is just words on paper is enough to help you deal with the problems you can encounter in the situations we describe. That has to be done by a real live person, face to face.

Don't shrug off or disregard the emotional problems that can go with an emergency situation. We both know from firsthand experience that even ambulance crews—people you'd expect to be totally case-hardened—suffer emotional upheavals from some of the things they have to deal with. The ambulance company we both had experience with provided a counselor for their people to talk to when that happened. More and more ambulance services are following suit.

If the people who deal on a day-to-day basis with the worst of emergencies can have problems, certainly you have the right to have emotional snags and mental pain and suffering.

Face it, admit it, talk to someone about it, get help in getting rid of it.

Chapter X

Handling a Long-term Stay

Let's face it, staying in a hospital is not really anybody's idea of a treat, even if just for a short time. But how do you handle knowing you are going to be there for a long haul without driving yourself and everyone around you totally nutty?

Young people are prone to some of the injuries that make a long stay necessary—multiple fractures from piling up a three-wheeler, for example. Bones don't heal in a hurry. Neither do burns. The effects of heart surgery heal slowly.

Attitude, of course, is the biggest thing you have going for you. It can be good or bad, but if it's bad it will work against not only you, but everyone you come in contact with.

Take it from a nurse, you don't—repeat DON'T—want your nurse mad at you.

Nurses, the same ones who take care of you and give you those shots and other unpleasant but necessary treatments—can be very good allies during your hospitalization. Nurses and other members of the medical team will take good care of you regardless of their feelings toward you. They are human, however, and it is difficult always to be nice and friendly toward someone who is at best unfriendly and at worst a brat they would probably secretly love to turn over a knee, cast or no cast.

If you are going to be in the hospital for a long time, by all means bring your own things whenever you can. If possible, wear your own pajamas or gowns. They're not only familiar but probably much more comfortable. A robe and slippers also make you feel more like getting out of your room whenever possible, and that will almost always be good for you.

Put up posters if they'll let you. If not on a wall, tape one to the door of your room. Bring some favorite pictures to set around the room. If you are in a private room it is easier to make it more "You."

Most hospital rooms are equipped with a TV, but the long-term stay is when you will almost surely want your own portable radio or tape player. (A pair of earphones would be considerate of other patients.)

Is there something you have always wanted to learn about or learn to do? We talked about that in Chapter VII, "How to Keep from Getting Bored Cross-eyed." It is especially good advice if you are going to be here a long time.

Consider "rewarding" yourself for a good day—a day when you didn't snarl at anyone, get weepy and depressed, or just generally give way to a bad attitude. For example, for every "good" day you might put a dollar in a special fund for yourself. Promise yourself to spend it on something extravagant and silly when you get out—dinner for yourself and a friend at the fanciest restaurant in town, five straight hours of video games, a piece of jewelry.

Having a goal or something to look forward to can do a lot to help you make it over the long haul.

In long hospital stays, it is easy to give way to a reaction psychologists call "displacement." We mentioned it in Chapter IX on being admitted through the emergency room. You are furious that you are hurt or sick and here in the first place, and you almost certainly can't hit out at whatever caused it, so you turn your fury on the handiest targets—usually your family and the medical staff.

You've done it. We've all done it. And if someone points out that the person you yelled at didn't *do* anything, you will almost certainly say, "Look, I've got a lot laid on me and I'm not in the best mood at the moment. When he/she kept clearing his throat/asked that stupid question/rattled the dishes while I was trying to watch TV, it was just the straw that broke the proverbial camel's vertebrae." Don't kid yourself. You are just taking out your anger on whoever happens to be around. And since you will probably see the most of your family, it's easiest to be nastiest to them.

They are going through a bad time now, too—don't you ever doubt it! So ease up, okay? Remember you can be sick or hurt and still be a creep.

Long-term hospital stays really are a problem. If you realize you are in for one, ask to talk to the hospital chaplain or a counselor. Tell him or her what is happening, that you realize some bad times may be ahead, and ask for advice on ways to deal with it.

The top line was attitude. So is the bottom line.

In the end, *you* are the one who will make or break things for yourself. (That statement is true where most of your life is concerned, come to think of it.)

You will almost certainly backslide—most people do. But if you determine you are going to make the best of it, not take your frustration out on other people, and if possible gain a new skill or area of knowledge, the time will pass much, *much* more quickly and more pleasantly for everyone.

But nobody can realistically ask you to be Pollyanna. Long-term stays do have some results that can be very unpleasant. (That was why we suggested talking to a professional about the problem.)

One result of prolonged confinement for anyone is depression. If you are completely immobile, such as in a body cast, one way to help this is to change your surroundings. Different posters, different bedspreads, even now and then, when possible, a change of room will help.

So will being as physically active as you are permitted to be. If you are allowed to exercise, find out what you can do, how much and how often you can do it, and then by all means exercise to the limits your doctor allows.

It will help you both physically and mentally.

If at all possible, get out of your room and see what is happening in the hospital world around you. Go for a wheelchair ride around the nurses' station and in the halls outside your room. Go to the visitors' lounge or down to the cafeteria or gift shop. Or all of the above.

If you can roll a wheelchair yourself, think of it as pumping iron! (It will be, after all!) If you can't, ask your nurse if someone will take you.

Go wherever you are allowed at least once a day and more often when possible. It helps to keep your room from becoming a dark cave of retreat with imaginary bars on the windows.

Television can be a wonderful diversion if you cannot

leave your bed or room, but if you are not a fan of the addled agonies of the soap operas or of game shows, you might have the family investigate the possibilities of bringing in a VCR and hooking it up to your television set—*after* you have obtained permission from the hospital engineers to do so. If it is possible, you have an almost endless variety of movies to choose for your entertainment.

Keep your mind busy, even if you have to force yourself. The worst thing you can do is lie and stare at the ceiling and brood.

Find out from your doctor what exercise is permitted, but remember that your doctor is the best judge here. Let him or her advise you, and do not overstep the limits you are given. It could hurt. It could make your long hospital stay even longer.

Chapter XI

Handling the Hassle of Checking In

If your admission to the hospital is scheduled, you will be able to take with you the information that the business office wants before sending you up to your room. Unless, of course, you really don't recall your great-great-grandmother's maiden name and where she was born.

Hospitals ask a lot of questions for your chart. Some make sense, but others make very little difference to anything having to do with your treatment.

Still, cooperate as best you can. People get very edgy answering all the questions, but hospitals do need a lot of information for your *safe* treatment. If yours is an "ordinary American" name, it is entirely possible that someone else with the same name has been treated at that hospital. Maybe more than one person. Even if your name is most unusual, you'd be surprised how often you'll find someone else sharing it.

If the hospital doesn't have further means of identification, such as your social security number if you have one, or your parents' names, that other person's chart might be pulled and sent to the nurses' station in place of yours. You could be given a medication to which you are allergic, or a medication that would help you could be withheld because your "alter ego" is allergic to it. Use of one patient's chart for another patient's treatment is something hospitals try very hard to guard against, so cooperate by answering all the questions as fully as you can. It really is in your best interest.

Important things you will need to have are, of course, your insurance information and the full addresses and telephone numbers of emergency contacts.

After you have finished in the admitting office, you may want your parents to go with you through the rest of the check-in procedure, or you may prefer to go alone. We believe that your wishes should be respected on this point.

You will probably have blood drawn and be asked to give a urine specimen for lab work. You will possibly have an X-ray made either before or shortly after you are assigned to a room.

The nurse who talks to you after you are in your room will ask questions specifically concerning your present physical condition and past medical and family medical history.

One of the most important things you will be asked is whether you have any allergies to food or medication. You should know that allergic reactions can be life-threatening, so this question must be answered to the best of your ability. (If you do have such an allergy, you should be wearing a necklace or bracelet containing that information along with any other serious medical conditions you have, such as diabetes.

You will probably be asked about allergies many times. Don't get impatient. It is for your own protection.

The nurse should also familiarize you with your room, how to call for a nurse when you need one, how to operate the television, raise and lower the bed, and so on. With the nurse, be sure everything is working as it should. One of the authors had an experience as a patient with a nurse-call that had not been plugged in or turned on and therefore did not operate.

If the staff knows the scheduling for your tests or surgery at the time of check-in, they can give you an idea of what to expect and when. However, these may not have been scheduled yet by your doctor.

One of the first things most teens do when finally left alone in their room is to call a few friends. It seems like a lifeline to the outside world, helping them feel they are not abandoned or cast adrift from the rest of the everyday world.

One last thing you need to understand from the beginning. Your physician's word is law. He or she writes orders for exactly what is to happen to you from the start. That includes what you eat, whether you can get out of bed and walk around, and what medicines you will be given.

Nurses, by law, can only follow these instructions in regard to your medical care. So if you have a problem with the doctor's orders, want to know the reason for them, or disagree with them, you need to talk to your doctor, not get angry with the nursing staff.

Chapter XII

Do You Need a New Face?

One of man's—and woman's—most basic fears is the fear of disfigurement. That's why "monsters" are so horrible-looking in scary movies. They represent a secret fear we all have that we'll end up like that some time.

What if you were burned or went face-first through a window and show it?

Your doctor should have talked with you about plastic and reconstructive surgery right from the beginning. But if he or she didn't, take heart.

New techniques have been developed within the last few years that give plastic surgery a whole new range of ways to rebuild faces, erase scars, and improve appearance after trauma.

According to Lori Hansen, M.D., of Oklahoma City, a plastic surgeon especially trained to work on the head and neck, "So much can be done now and done on an outpatient basis. Of course, in the case of trauma it's usually better if the reconstruction is begun right away, but even if you have old scars and old problems, you should talk with a plastic surgeon and see what can be done."

(Dr. Hansen is a former Miss Oklahoma and a beauty herself. Whenever anyone calls cosmetic or plastic surgery a "vanity operation" she says, "I don't see it that way at all. I think God means for us to win in life, and the better we look, the better we feel about ourselves. The better we feel about ourselves, the happier and more successful we will be!")

We have heard of parents who didn't want to pay for plastic surgery if it wasn't covered by insurance, saying, "Don't worry so much about how you look. People will love you for what's on the inside, for the person you really are." We wrote a book about that (*Coping with Your Image,* Rosen Publishing Group) and how important the way you look and feel about yourself is to your life now and your career later.

So if you do need plastic or reconstructive surgery, try as hard as you can to get it. It will make a tremendous difference in your life.

(As a personal prejudice on the part of one of the authors, if the work needed is on your head and neck, see a surgeon who was especially trained to work on that area. The results generally seem to be better.)

But what if all the scars and all the trauma can't be erased?

That's a tough one to live with, but some very successful people have done it. You will have to try harder and work harder, but in most cases you still can go wherever you want in life.

The key is not to let yourself be bitter about it. Burn scars may not put people off nearly as much as an angry, bitter attitude, or martyrdom, or "Poor little me, make it up to me for the bad things that have happened to me." Any of those put people off, badly enough to hurt your getting along with them more than the scars and aftereffects of whatever happened to you.

Chapter XIII

When Someone Else Was Responsible for What Happened

We have talked about displacement, when you can't hit out at whoever caused what happened to you.

But what about when you *can*, when it was directly someone else's fault?

Fault, blame, and guilt are an emotional tarbaby that can really snarl you up inside, to the point of hindering your progress in getting better.

Especially when those feelings are aimed at yourself!

For example, you were driving and you "only" lost a hand. Your best friend was killed. You can feel as if somebody set off an emotional atomic bomb in your brain.

Or maybe you were doing absolutely nothing but walking home from school and you never even saw the car with the drunk driver at the wheel until it jumped the curb and hit you, leaving you with critical injuries and facing a long, painful convalescence. Thinking about the person at the wheel, right now you *know* you are fully capable of murder.

Don't expect those feelings to die down overnight or even quickly. You'd be less than human if they did. And don't let other people tell you how to feel: "You have to forgive and forget and get on with your life."

(You do, as a matter of fact, but having people say that to you isn't likely to help the process get started.)

Give yourself a little time to get over the first emotional explosion, and then talk to a professional counselor about your feelings. And that goes even if you were at fault. Many people feel that if something was their fault, they *should* suffer and be miserable to "pay" for what they did. That's nonsense! Talk to a professional therapist about it.

Try to get your family to do so as well. Something like this can be devastating to the whole family. According to seventeen-year-old Tina, who was badly injured when the car in which she was riding was hit by a drunk driver, "The damage it did to me was much less than the damage it did to my family.

"Mother was at the hospital all the time. The rest of the family almost never saw her unless they came up there. When she did spend time with them, she was raging about how the man who did this should get the electric chair or at the very least life in prison. She was just obsessed with 'getting' him. She'd go on and on and on! You got tired of hearing about it.

"My dad didn't know how to cope with it. Mother was after him for not being as eaten up with 'nailing' the driver as she was, for being able to spend time doing and thinking about other things. He didn't know how to cope with my spending six months in a wheelchair and having to go through all the things I did when I was in physical therapy and starting to walk again and all that. So he just started staying away, working late every night and weekends at the office.

"My little sister started having nightmares, and my brother got into fights at school—the family was falling apart. It was really awful. One day I asked if I could visit our minister, and I told him what was happening and asked if he could help. He saw us all together, then separately, and things started to get better. But it was really rough on us all. I mean, I was seeing my mom and dad heading for a divorce, the way they were acting to each other."

You may have a perfect right to feel fury at someone else for what happened. No one could logically deny that. But negative emotion uses up a lot of drive and energy, and while you may not have the saintlike ability to totally forgive and forget, it's in your own best interest to channel your feelings into getting well and getting on with your life.

Get someone to help you do that if you need to.

A friend of one of the authors, Dan Case, of Oklahoma City, as a youngster was struck by a hit-and-run driver, with internal injuries so severe that surgeons had to remove his spleen.

"I never even saw the car," he says today. "I was going across the street to play with my brother, and the next thing I remember was waking up in a hospital room, tied down, with tubes in my arms, side, and mouth. I couldn't see anyone I knew, and I had no idea what had happened to me.

"I can still remember exactly how scared I was, what a really terrifying experience it was."

The driver went to another hospital, confessed what she had done, and had a nervous collapse. Later she faced the Case family and also visited Dan in the hospital, bringing him a present and telling him that she had hit him and how sorry she was.

"My parents told me it was an accident, that she

didn't mean to do it, and I could accept that and just go on from there. But even so, something like that affects the whole family. It certainly did all of us."

Chapter XIV

The Toughest Part

If you are one of the people to whom the "in for a long stay" chapters apply, you are almost surely going to spend time in some type of rehabilitation, usually physical therapy.

That can be the hardest part of getting over your accident or illness because, more than in almost any other situation, your mental and physical capacities and abilities will be at war with each other and with outside influences, pulled apart in a dozen directions.

"Rehabilitation is really rough," according to Isobel Knoepfli, head of the Department of Physical Therapy at the Goddard Health Center of the University of Oklahoma. "For one thing, by the time a young person gets this far, the first shock of what happened has worn off and his or her emotions are much more pronounced. They swing from rebellion to anger to depression and back again, and sometimes the patient feels more than one, or all of them at the same time."

Physical therapy can be painful, and it involves a lot of plain, hard, sweaty work. Sometimes the gains are tiny, and sometimes you see no results for what seems the longest time in the world.

In some cases the patient is almost back to the stage of infancy, having to relearn the things a baby learns.

Anger and indignation are natural results of such a setback, but they can also get in the way of the determination needed for real progress.

"Some people say, either to themselves or out loud, that they 'refuse to accept' what has happened to them, as if it were a package they were returning to the sender," Ms. Knoepfli says.

"If you are in a wheelchair and the doctors don't think you have a real chance to walk again, or you have lost a leg or an arm, you *have* to accept it and start rebuilding your life around it."

"Refusing to accept" something like that is often considered admirable, worthy of praise, showing courage and determination. It isn't. That is, refusing to accept the fact that it happened to you isn't a virtue. It is being afraid to face the facts.

"Refusing to accept" that it can stop you from leading the best life you can and working around whatever happened *is* courage of the highest order.

Maybe you are in a wheelchair or have lost an arm or a leg, but there is still a *lot* you can do with your life and with your future.

"One real problem about rehabilitation is that the mental and the physical ability and drive may not match," the physical therapist says. "You may have all the mental determination in the world to get in there and work your tail off, but physically you are just not at the stage where you can do it. And often, when you can't do what you want to make yourself better, you slide into a downer, and by the time you are physically able to start the long road back, mentally you lack the will to make your body get out there and do it.

"The physical and mental ability not being in step is

one of the biggest problems faced by someone going through rehabilitation."

You may have to change your life-style. But if you look around there are likely to be more things you can do than you might think, even if you do have limitations, either temporary or permanent.

Remember the girl in the TV movie "Skyward"? She was in a wheelchair, yet she learned to fly an airplane. You can, too, if you want to. You can drive a car or go to medical or law school. All kinds of doors are out there. You just have to open them.

One thing you can and *must* do is keep other people from making you more helpless than you already are. Family and friends—and total strangers—because they feel sorry for you and perhaps because they feel a little (or a lot) guilty over what happened, have a horrible tendency to want to do things for you, wait on you hand and foot, make your life "easier." A little pampering is nice now and again. But notice we said a *little*. A lot, just sitting back and letting others do things you are perfectly able to do for yourself, can turn you into a blubbering baby.

A friend of one of the authors is an excellent case in point. When he was seventeen he fell off the roof of the family home, hitting a metal meter box and so totally shattering a leg that it had to be amputated.

His parents felt terribly guilty; they had sent him up to adjust the antenna of the TV, over his protests. So they waited on him, coddled and pampered and protected him, fussed over his food and whether he was warm enough or cool enough. In a very short time an athletic, intelligent young man had become a spoiled and helpless child again.

From then on, his life and his world revolved around his health problems and all the things he *couldn't* do. He had passed the examination to get into medical school, but he didn't go and ended with a low-paying, no-future job. He lost a lot of friends, several girlfriends, and eventually his wife, because everyone got fed to the back teeth with his self-centered "poor little me."

"When you're around Marvyn," a former girlfriend said, "all you talk about is 'poor Marvyn' and is his leg hurting, is it time to take his medicine, does he need a laxative—yes, really!—and other aspects of his health. It doesn't take long to bore you blue in the face. Marrying Marvyn would be like taking on a thirty-year-old baby!"

Don't snarl at people who offer to carry your books, push your wheelchair, cut up your food for you. They are trying to be kind. But if you can do it yourself, do it.

And that can be terribly hard, as hard as the daily exercises and work in physical therapy. It's so easy not to do the things you need to do, so much simpler to let it slide "just this once," so much less hassle to let other people do things for you and to skip your exercises. When the realization comes that you should be in square four on the road back and there you are, sitting like a bullfrog in square one, the depression, the anger at yourself and others, the realization that it's going to be that much harder to get started again, can be a burden so overwhelming that you don't even have the will to try to pick it up and carry it.

It's easier to sit back and snivel and feel sorry for yourself.

As you are going through rehabilitation, you need to

be able to talk with your doctor and with your therapist. Therapy is not a cut-and-dried thing. People respond at vastly different rates to the business of getting better. But you should be able to get answers as to what you can expect and what you can do to get yourself back. Vague replies and no real information are no more helpful here—and they can be more depressing—than in any other area of medicine.

Work like blazes, but don't overdo it. If the doctor says twenty exercises, doing forty won't be twice as good. Overdoing can weaken muscles not ready for such stress and can set you back, not put you forward.

So work, but follow orders, too.

"Rehabilitation can do wonders," Ms. Knoepfli says. "But nobody can do it for you. It's your personal responsibility. In the end it's up to you. You have to take the first steps and keep on going."

How do you eat a whale?

One bite at a time.

Here's a knife and fork—get on with it!

Chapter XV

Getting Back to the World

Getting out of the hospital and "back to the world"—to use the Vietnam-era phrase—can be traumatic in itself, and the longer you were a patient, the more likely that is to be true.

You may have physical limitations. You may feel like a different person. You may even *look* like a different person. Going back to school that first day can be the hardest thing you ever did.

How is the best way to handle it?

There is really no one "best" way. You might want to ask a couple of friends to go with you. You might go very early, so you can already be in your classroom when the morning stampede starts. If you will need special help, talk to your school counselor about it beforehand.

People seem to react to being in the hospital in one of two ways—either not wanting to talk about it at all, or finding themselves talking about it a lot.

If you don't want to talk about it, that's certainly your right, and you should let other people know from the beginning how you feel.

If you do want to talk about it, remember that people who go on and on about "my operation" are the subject of a lot of jokes and cartoons. It's a natural thing to happen, really. It was the most interesting thing that happened to you, and it certainly had an effect on your life. Probably you will find yourself talking about it quite a lot to your friends.

Just watch out that you don't become a rousing bore on the subject. It's so easy to do! Your hospitalization probably got you a lot of special attention, made you a center of interest, and it's easy to want to take advantage of that fact and prolong it. But eventually it will work to your disadvantage. So be careful.

Do follow doctor's orders! If he said don't play football for six weeks, you are risking being flat on your back staring at a hospital ceiling again if you do. Don't feel that you have to prove anything. You will really be furious with yourself if you wind up back in Room 203 just because you had to be macho.

It's really surprising how often people, especially young people, think that just because they feel okay, everything is the way it was before the hospital stay.

Be prepared for sudden spells of feeling weak and tired. You probably won't really hurt or feel sick, but just suddenly as if someone had pulled the energy plug. Rest! At the very least, sit down for a while. Your body is telling you something. Listen to it. To overdo is to risk slowing down the work of healing, making complete recovery take that much longer.

The emphasis these days is on getting the patient out of the hospital as quickly as possible. At one time someone having an appendectomy stayed in the hospital and in bed from one to three weeks. Now it's rare to be in for more than three days. But that also means that your body still has a long way to go to get up to full steam. So give it time. Don't push.

Do what the doctors told you, and don't overdo anything.

Of course, there's the happy possibility that you will go back to the world in far better shape than when you entered the hospital. Perhaps surgery has corrected a heart defect that severely limited your life. Or you now have a working kidney instead of having to depend on dialysis.

If that applies to you, you also may be tempted to "push," to overdo just to show you are "all right." If you have lived with a long-standing problem, you know how important doctor's orders are. Just because you feel better than you have in years, don't overdo now just because you can.

As with so many other things in this book, if you find yourself having any real problems going back to the world, back to school, and back into your everyday life, get help. Talk to someone about it, a professional someone who can offer real help, not just opinions.

It really can make a difference.

Chapter XVI

"If You've Got Cancer, Are You Gonna Croak?"

Until the last few years, young people with serious medical problems were rarely seen by the general public or by their peers. They were isolated in special classes, taught in hospitals, kept apart. But recently the trend has been to "mainstream" them, put them in regular classes, make their lives as normal as possible. While that has a lot going for it, the person most directly concerned—the patient—also can expect some bad moments.

According to Tom, a Midwestern seventeen-year-old who lost most of his left leg in a boating accident, "Not many adults handled meeting me for the first time after it happened, and *no* kids did. People just didn't know how to talk to me or what to say. Either they tried to act like nothing had happened, or they asked all kinds of questions I really didn't want to answer right then—like 'What did you feel like when you saw your leg was gone?' You'd think people would know better than to come up with dumb things like that, but I heard it a lot.

"I finally learned to say, 'How do you think you'd feel if it happened to you, and how do you think you'd feel if somebody asked you a question like that about it?' Usually they'd stop and look sort of stupid and then say, 'Yeah, I guess that was kind of dumb to say, wasn't it?' "

Jenny has had cancer, and the doctors say that her chances now look good. Her hair is growing back, and she is putting on some weight. After her initial treatments, she attended school with her regular class.

"It didn't even bother me the first time somebody said, 'If you have cancer, are you gonna croak?' because someone was *talking* to me! When I went back to school I was rail skinny and had on this awful wig that looked like I'd gotten it from the Three Stooges—and people looked right through me. Some of my best friends! I had to look in a mirror to be sure I wasn't invisible!

"I understand it; they didn't know what to say or were afraid of saying the wrong thing. But it felt awful to be ignored like that, and I'd go home and cry. Finally I decided I was just going to ignore being ignored. The next day I spoke to everyone I knew by name. I didn't try to stop them or start a conversation or anything. I'd just say something like, 'Hi, Ann, I like that sweater,' or 'Hello, Alec, you sure gave an interesting report on Air Force fighter airplanes,' and go on. Everybody acted really startled at first, but because I didn't stop I didn't make them uncomfortable.

"I started speaking up in class like I always had—teachers were looking right through me, too—and pretty soon I found I was being accepted by more and more people. One day I gave a report in class about the treatments. Not about just what happened to me, but what they can do for cancer patients in general. After that the worst was over, because I didn't act like I wanted pity or anything."

Like most young people with medical problems, Jenny developed a tolerance of dumb questions. "No question is really dumb, I guess. Most people ask things because they want to know, and when it comes to something like cancer most people don't know very much. Sometimes questions hurt, but if they do, I let the person know. Sometimes I feel like questions are meant to hurt, like the person is needling you. Just hand it back is what I do.

"If someone's being tacky to me, I don't have any hesitation to be tacky back. But if someone really wants to know, that's something else. The way to get along is to act as normal as you can and, as much as you can, refuse to be treated any differently than anyone else. Something happened to part of me, but I—me inside—am still the same person I always was."

Chapter XVII

A Psychiatric Hospitalization: Not What You Probably Think

There can be many, many reasons for a teen to have a psychiatric hospitalization. Alcohol problems and drug problems are two of them. Emotional problems of the patient or emotional problems at home that make it impossible to get along with other family members are two others. Teens with self-destructive behavior patterns—stealing, truancy, constant problems in school—are sometimes candidates for a psychistric hospital admission. Many teens ask to be admitted to such a hospital or unit.

(The real, outright "craziness"—hearing voices, seeing things, thinking they are Julius Caesar, being totally out of touch with reality—is very rare in young people.)

Long ago psychiatric hospitals were almost all "snake pits"—grim, drab, depressing places where patients rarely ever got out. In those terrible days the first thing that was done to patients was to shave their head. If you were not whacko when you got in, you were almost guaranteed to be off the rails after you had been there a while.

But things have changed dramatically for the better. Now it is understood how important environment is to helping a patient get better. The psychiatric unit may be the most cheerful and comfortable one in a hospital. The length of the average psychiatric hospitalization, for any age group, is under a month. And the majority of people who are released in that short a time never go back.

What can you expect of a psychiatric hospitalization? That depends a great deal on the hospital. If possible, choose a hospital with an adolescent unit, where you will be with other kids, or one like Oklahoma City's Willow View Hospital, which is a psychiatric hospital primarily for (although not limited to) adolescent patients.

Since you won't be physically sick and unable to get around, your surroundings are particularly important to you here. Ask what kind of things, including clothes, you can bring from home to make your room as pleasant and cheerful as possible. If it is during the school year, be prepared for the hospital to help you make some arrangements to continue your studies and keep up in school. (Most such large units or hospitals have their own program of instruction.)

Expect, of course, to meet other kids your age, and older and younger. You may be surprised at how many other people or families have the same kind of problem that is tearing you or your family to pieces. The patients sometimes learn as much from each other about how to deal with things as they do from the therapists.

You will probably spend some time talking to a psychiatrist. Most kids have a wrong idea of what it is like to talk to a psychiatrist. They expect a funny little man with a beard and a Viennese accent who is a little bit cuckoobird himself and demands to know all their innermost secrets and thoughts and ideas.

Certainly there are poor psychiatrists, just as there are poor representatives of every profession. But the good psychiatrists—and that is most of them—won't scare you, embarrass you, or make you wish you were on the dark side of the moon. Most therapists, whether they are psychologists or psychiatrists, begin by getting to know you and helping you relax and learn to trust them. Probably at first you will talk privately with a therapist and also be part of a group session.

The idea of "group therapy" scares a lot of teens. They say, "I don't want to tell my secrets to people or talk about what's wrong in my life in front of a bunch of strangers!"

Relax! To begin with, you won't have to say anything you don't want to say. That should be obvious. Second, everyone there has problems, too, or they wouldn't be part of your group. You will also find that many of those problems are more serious or more dangerous than yours. Third, teens in a psychiatric hospital tend to develop an attitude of, "We're all in this together and we all need to help each other." It's more likely that the people you meet will be helpful and protective than that anything you say will be used to hurt you by other patients.

You may worry about what other kids or other people in general will think of you for being here. After all, think of all the names we have for a psychiatric hospital—the funny farm, the loony bin, the laughing academy, the crazy house.

We aren't saying that won't be a problem. It may very well be. There are geeks in this world who, once anyone has had an emotional problem or a psychiatric hospitalization, forever after see that person as a candidate for a straitjacket. Which is pure garbage.

Talk to your doctor about this. Get his or her help if it is or may be a problem.

A lot has been said in recent years about things like employment applications that say, "Have you ever been hospitalized for a psychiatric problem?" And of course anyone honest enough to check the "yes" box had the chance of an igloo at the equator of getting the job.

Again, talk to your doctor about this. (Some of them say, "Lie. Check no. This has nothing to do with your ability to do a good job.")

What about your friends and family?

Let's take family first. With a psychiatric hospitalization families seem to fall into one of three categories. First are the ones who see the problem, are loving and supportive, and really want to help. If they think this is the best thing for you, they are behind you one hundred percent.

Unfortunately, that is the rarest group.

Another category is the family that expects the hospital to do what they have been unwilling or unable to do: solve the kid's problems and change his or her behavior.

According to a psychologist who specializes in adolescent patients, "Of course, even good parents, parents and families that have done all the right things and none of the wrong ones, sometimes turn out a kid who is a problem, a hellion bent on destroying his own life as well as making everyone else around him totally miserable.

"But much of the time parents with a kid who has a

problem have done something to contribute to it. Sometimes it is something they couldn't help, like a divorce or serious illness in the family. But sometimes parents are just 'too busy,' too wrapped up in their careers to really *be* parents. So when the kid starts getting into trouble and having problems, they take him to a psychiatrist or psychologist or want him admitted to a hospital. The attitude is sort of, 'Here. This kid is "broke." "Fix" him for me and send me the bill.'

"One family member with problems severe enough to be helped by hospitalization affects all the family. And rarely do things get better in a case like that. To make them get better, the whole family has to try to make them better. Parents can't often just hand a kid over to a hospital and have *them* straighten everything out."

The third type of family is the one that turns inside out at the mere *idea* that anyone from "our family could *possibly* have a...a...*mental* problem!"

That, too, is common. The way these people see it, if *he* has a problem, that means *they* did something wrong or that something might be wrong with them, and these tend to be the people who have never done anything wrong in their lives. (Ha!) Children themselves in such a situation sometimes ask to go to a psychiatric unit, and the parents are immediately up on their hind legs at the idea.

Talk to your therapist about your family and their roles in your life and whatever has you here. Don't be afraid or embarrassed. More and more therapists are learning just how destructive the effects of certain families can be on various members.

(If you are interested, you might read two books on

pathological families and how unsolved family problems led to tragedy. Both are true. One is *Bad Blood*, the story of a California teenager whose battles with her alcoholic mother and problems with her wishy-washy father who wouldn't make decisions in the face of a family crisis led her to egg her boyfriend into murdering her parents. In *Nutcracker*, by Shana Alexander, a mentally ill and abusive mother pushed and brainwashed her seventeen-year-old son into murdering her own father. Admittedly, such cases are rare. But living in a disturbed family is unfortunately not so uncommon, and the effects can be terrible.)

For a long time psychiatric units or hospitals were "revolving doors"—patients came in, got better, were sent back into the same family or same environment, and everything went wrong all over again. Psychiatrists were very reluctant to "play God" by saying, "You need to get away from that family! You need to get out of that environment!"

Now they are more realistic, and it is helping patients more all the time. If a home environment is bad, if the parents are the real root of the problem, therapists can do a lot to change the whole situation, not just one person's role or place in it.

(Some states have "emancipated minors" laws. Teens from a bad home situation who have demonstrated that they are mature and stable enough to live on their own can be declared "emancipated," giving them much the same legal status as an adult. Such a standing has to be granted by a court of law, but if the family situation is at fault and you can get along on your own, consider this possibility if it is available in your state.)

A psychiatric hospitalization can help. Emotional problems can hurt as much as physical ones. They can mess up your life just as badly. They can ruin the present *and* the future.

For the kid who is sick to death of being drunk, tired to the core of his soul of always being in trouble, and yet is not able to break the pattern, or who is caught up in an impossible home situation that is pushing him or her to the breaking point, consider the possibility of a psychiatric hospitalization or at least psychiatric help.

It might save your life, or at least your happiness and your future.

Speaking is Tina, sixteen, and a junior in high school.

"Home has been the pits for almost as long as I can remember. Dad is a workaholic; he's *never* around, always at the office. Mom is an *alcoholic*. Usually she was sloshed by the time any of us kids got home from school.

"My big sister had a baby her senior year in high school. Mom and Dad wanted to kick her out, but they didn't, and now she and the kid live at home. She doesn't work, and she expects everyone else to take care of her little boy. My two little brothers are always in trouble at school.

"Home is nothing but fighting and yelling and screaming. Walking home after school, I'd find my stomach pulling into a knot because I dreaded so much walking in the door. I thought a lot about suicide, I was so unhappy."

Tina's behavior began showing signs of trouble, too. She was arrested twice for shoplifting and was more and more often in trouble at school. One day her counselor suggested that Tina be admitted to a psychiatric unit for adolescents.

"It really scared me at first," she admits. "I thought, 'The loony bin! No way I'd do a thing like that!' But the more I thought it over, the more I realized I did want to go, if only to get away from the screaming and uproar, to be somewhere where it was quiet and peaceful and I could just lie down and read or watch TV. So I asked my dad if he'd sign the papers."

She looks out the window, and there is a long silence. "Man, I was scared to death that first day. I had this 'One flew over the cuckoo's nest' idea, and I didn't know if I'd ever be let out again. I was shaking when my doctor walked me to the door.

"Instead of being full of 'crazy people,' the hospital was full of kids a lot like me with problems a lot like mine. It was a real surprise. When you are as unhappy as I was, it's easy to think everybody else in the world and every family in the world has it good and things like this don't happen to them. In a way it was a relief to learn they do.

"And it really helped me learn to cope with things. I found out that the way I acted, or reacted, when Mom got on one of her tirades was just making things worse.

"I saw kids with worse problems than I had and they were managing to handle things and were determined that their lives weren't going to be ruined. It made me determined, too."

Another silence. "I saw kids who *knew* they were screwing up their own lives but just wouldn't stop what they were doing. I started thinking, 'That's stupid, man! Maybe you are getting back at your mother, but it's *you* that's going to wind up in jail, dummy!' I decided I didn't want to do anything that stupid!"

"Being in the hospital *helped*! It really did. Not a lot has changed as far as my family and home go, but I can cope with it a whole lot better. I know in another year I'll be out of school and on my own, and I can get away and make a good life for myself then. Just knowing things are going to get better then is enough to let me hold on now when the screaming starts.

"Going back to school was really rough. Of course, the hospital didn't tell anyone I'd been there, and my doctor said I could tell my friends I'd been away in a private school for a short time or something like that. But most of my friends knew.

"There were one or two creeps who said things, but almost none of my real friends held it against me. They knew what a miserable home life I led and how unhappy I was, and they figured if it helped, that was all that mattered.

"If people weren't my friends, they were going to think I'd been in the loony bin, but it never mattered to me before what people who weren't my friends thought, so I decided not to let it matter now.

"I'd advise any kid with problems like I had to get help! Talk to a counselor. Don't have a fit if he or she suggests putting you in a hospital for a while. Anything to keep you from really making a mess of your life.

"I'd tell anyone, don't be afraid of being in a hospital like I was. It helps. It really does help!"

Chapter XVIII

When Things Are Not Going to Be "All Right"

The hospital is for getting better, getting well, fixing what's broke, curing diseases, solving problems. Would that it always could.

But sometimes it can't. Some diseases have no cure. Some accidents break and tear things that doctors can't fix. Burns leave you with lifelong scars and pain. Some diseases may or may not be cured; cancer is a big killer of young people, and the young cancer patient knows that he or she may, or may not, have a future.

How do you cope with such a situation?

According to the Rev. Bob Gardenhire III, Minister of Pastoral Care of the Church of the Servant (United Methodist), in Oklahoma City, one of the first things you need to do is open and keep open a line of communication with your family. "Such young patients typically think, 'Can I count on my folks for support? Will they not try to protect me or lie to me? Will they tell me what's really going on?'

"I think it's very important that everyone involved be honest with each other—and the protecting works both ways. Children want to protect their parents as much as parents want to shield their children from painful truths. Young patients may put on a terrific front of feeling great, conceal symptoms, or just not talk about the illness or injury because they know it will hurt the parents. They try to protect their parents from their sickness or pain as the parents may try to protect them from the truth.

"So openness and honesty work both ways."

Self-image and getting along with others come into play, too, in dealing with a "not going to be all right" situation. As we mentioned in Chapter XVI, being in an ordinary setting with a disability or a serious illness is rough. The Rev. Gardenhire says:

"One thing you can do is ask yourself, 'What have I felt or would I feel about someone who had lost a leg? How would I feel about someone who had terrible scars? To me, were they worth any less as persons because of that?'

"So often, when people are honest with themselves, they'll admit they don't think any less of someone else because of a physical problem. And if you do think less of someone, if you do see the person as having less value as a human being, stop and try to understand *why*. Are those really valid reasons? Probably not. If someone judged you the same way, how would you think and feel about that person? Looking at it from that angle can help you gain a whole different view of things.

"If the problem is life-threatening, you should try not to dwell on the uncertainty of your future, but instead think, 'How do I make today count? And what can I do with the future I really have?'

"Then create a new future for yourself."

If you know there's a chance you may not be around to graduate from college, creating a new future for yourself may mean being the most outstanding high school student you can possibly be. If you may not be here to have children of your own someday, spend time now as a volunteer teaching a Sunday School class or helping out in a children's hospital.

It's trite and a cliché and all that, but it is also true, that helping other people does a lot to make you feel good *and* take your mind off your own troubles.

"Make today count," the Rev. Gardenhire says. "Have a goal for each day. What about, 'Today I want to be a person who makes other people's day worthwhile?' That takes the focus off 'me' and moves it to other people, to a more positive and helpful viewpoint."

What about when people do lie to you? It can be very hard to handle, because we want so badly to believe that what they say is really true. Yet most people in such a situation know, even if it's very deep within, what the truth is. And for most of us, facing that truth is, in the long run, easier to handle and less stressful than deceiving ourselves.

"If you think people aren't being open and honest with you, say to them, 'What if I'm not going to be all right? Can we talk about that?' Very often teens—or anyone—can be very reluctant to do that because, as I said, the instinct to protect works both ways. But generally, getting things out into the open so that everyone knows what is going on and where they stand and what is likely to happen is the better solution."

When you do feel like talking about yourself and your problems, do find someone who will listen. "It can be your doctor, the hospital chaplain, your minister, a favorite teacher, a sympathetic cleaning woman! Whoever it is, when you are faced with that kind of thing you need to be able to get things off your chest."

"And for you, is God a part of this? Whatever religious point of view you come from, a great deal of help and strength and peace of mind is there."

The Rev. Gardenhire advises you to make your hospital room as much "yours" as possible. "It should be something of home, not an alien environment. That alone can make things easier for you."

"Be careful of sympathy and of feeling sorry for yourself. Instead of the friends who wail about poor little you, look for people who won't let you be Poor Pitiful Pearl but will kick you in the butt and push you to get out and do what you can when you can. Seek friends who will boot you out of a rut, instead of being scared that if you walk across the room you may have a heart attack right in front of them. Hang on to images and people that will help you get where you are going."

In the case of a great many things that could come in this category—perhaps you are in a wheelchair now—you must face the fact that things are going to be different and that it's perfectly natural and all right to worry about what adults may see as "minor" problems: "How can I run around now? Who's going to be my friend? Will anybody ever ask me for a date? Do I dare ask anyone for a date? What if I miss a lot of school? Can I graduate with the kids I've always known?"

Friends can help a lot here. "Keep in touch," the Rev. Gardenhire advises. "Ask them for advice in handling these kinds of worry. They may have solutions and ideas that haven't occurred to you. Keep in touch with friends. Go out of your way to keep communication open and friendship strong."

A way to help keep the lines open between you and friends is to make people enjoy staying in touch with you. Self-pity, blame, anger, giving up, feeling sorry for yourself, talking at great length about the things you can't do anymore or your bleak future or what you have lost makes people people feel uncomfortable, uneasy, perhaps even guilty. The natural result of such feelings? Think about it yourself. If you are uncomfortable being around someone, you tend not to be around them any more than you can help.

"You can get bitter, or you can get better," the minister says.

"Don't be afraid to ask for what you want or need. If you want company, friendship, emotional support, help with homework, a ride to the ballgame—don't be afraid to ask. Don't feel you have to 'prove' something by never needing help. We all need help sometimes."

Be open with your doctor. You do have rights in this matter. Ask for honesty and straightforwardness. And be willing to be a partner in your own progress, not just someone who sits back and watches everything happening to him or her. Be able to say, "Okay, doc, if that's the situation thanks for leveling with me. Now, what can I do to make it better?" Patients who do that and really work at having the best life possible fare far better than those who simply wring their hands and moan.

"Realize, too, that your parents may be having problems handling your illness or accident because, as well as loving you and being upset about you, they also feel guilty." the Rev. Gardenhire says. "They may be feeling guilty because you got an undeserved spanking when you were six, because this happened to you and not to them, or because they feel something they did contributed to its happening at all. Or all of the above.

"Guilt is a painful and warping emotion. If you can understand that and bring it out into the open with them, you can very likely help them deal with things in a more positive, less painful way.

"Coping with a situation like this, when your future is uncertain, when you don't know that everything is going to be all right, or maybe you even know it *isn't* going to be, is really tough. But I think, as a general rule, kids can do it. Teens, on the whole, have more courage and more resiliency than adults. If they really try, they can handle it."

Chapter XIX

Avoiding the Hospital in the First Place

Accidents are the biggest killers and injurers of young people. Young people are mobile, active, too often incautious, and very inclined to push themselves beyond the limit by doing risky things to prove to themselves they can do it, to show off for their friends, or just because that's the way kids are.

And, of course, something bad is never going to happen to *you*, is it? It's always going to be the other guy.

We aren't against taking risks. We have done so and will in the future. The human race wouldn't have got very far if our ancestors had sat with their backs to the cave wall and been afraid to risk anything. We'd never have got off the ground or to the moon without taking risks.

But there are risks worth taking and risks that just aren't very smart.

One of the hardest parts of being hurt in an accident is knowing you were doing something silly that wasn't worth the risk you were taking. As we mentioned in Chapter IX on being responsible for what happened, the realization that if you hadn't done something ridiculous you wouldn't be here now can load you with emotional problems as hard to deal with as the physical ones.

You know what is dangerous. It doesn't take a genius to figure that out.

Don't drive like a bloody fool, no matter how it charges up your adrenalin and makes you look super cool. Don't drink and drive or ride with a drinking driver. Don't take *silly* risks. The price you can pay is like paying for diamonds and getting fish-tank gravel. That's too expensive in anyone's language.

To quote the classic admonition given to pilots at the briefing before an air show:

DON'T DO NUTHIN' DUMB.

Chapter XX

DIARY OF A HOSPITAL STAY

Saturday evening

I've always said I wanted to be a writer and write world-famous books that make megabucks, so I guess this is going to be good practice. Like I've always heard it said, I might as well do something like this—I can't dance. That's for sure! At least not for the next few months.

I'll start at the beginning. My name is David Lindsey. I'm sixteen years old and a junior in high school. And until a few days ago I lived what I guess you'd call a normal life, without very much excitement in it.

I sure didn't like the kind of excitement I got!

Last Wednesday afternoon I had to stay late at school to help decorate the gym for a dance, and Rodney Black offered me a ride home.

We were driving down the big hill from the high school, talking and listening to his radio, when I heard him yell as we went into the intersection on the highway.

I turned around to look over my shoulder and just got a glimpse of a truck coming right at me. All I could see was grille. I mean, man, like giant teeth or something.

The next thing I remember is someone talking to me

and telling me not to move, to try to be still.

It was a girl with long hair that kept blowing in her face, wearing some kind of a blue uniform. Not a police uniform, but a uniform of some kind.

I was kind of half in Rodney's car or what was left of Rodney's car, and there seemed to be a lot of people around me and a lot of noise. The main thing, though, was that I knew my legs were caught and that they hurt.

I found out later that it look almost an hour to cut me loose. They brought the thing the ambulance people call "Jaws." It's like a great big can opener and that's what it does to a car, just cuts it apart like a can. Rodney and the other people who saw it say it was really weird-looking.

But I only remember parts of it—people talking and screeching at me, and once seeing a TV camera looking almost into my face and the ambulance people getting mad about that. They put splints on both my legs and finally got me in the ambulance. I also remember hearing the sirens and being taken out at the hospital.

None of it is very clear, though. It's mainly just a blur of lights in my face and pain and noise and people around me.

The next thing I remember is waking up in a strange room with my right leg up in traction and a needle stuck in my arm and taped down and one of those bottles—they call them intravenous or IV bottles—hanging on this pole thing by the bed. There were wires on my chest that led to this thing they said was a heart monitor, and it made a beeping sound every time my heart beat.

It was all pretty weird, but just as I was starting to

freak and trying to get loose from some of the stuff, I saw my parents were there and that calmed me down a lot.

Then a nurse came in and told my parents what all the things were that I was hooked up to. I wasn't even sure how the accident happened. I mean, I was there, for sure, but it was all blurry. (Later I remembered it all very clearly, but right then I didn't.)

My parents said that a big truck, almost as big as an 18-wheeler, had run the light and hit us broadside. The jerk who was driving the truck (that wasn't even damaged very much) threw a big fit and kept saying "Did you see that! Stupid kids ran right through that light! It's sure not *my* fault!" You know how it goes—when anything like that happens it's always the kid who's in the wrong. But a lot of people saw this and told the police it wasn't Rodney's fault, so I guess that's good.

Rod wasn't hurt that bad; he's more scratched and cut up than I am and has a broken arm. But the nurse said the ambulance people told her he thought I was dead, and he was more upset about that than anything else. It made me feel really funny—I mean, your best friend thinking you are dead! Then Mom started to cry and Dad got all embarrassed and I wished the nurse had never mentioned it.

Anyway, I had a concussion and a broken leg. The nurse called it a fracture of the femur, the big bone they call the thigh bone. They took me from the emergency room to surgery, where they put a pin through the bone to hold it still while it's in traction.

Above and around the bed there's all this stuff—rope pulls and weights, and tubes and wires and all sorts of things. I feel like I'm wired for sound or belong in the Houston Space Center or something.

I'll have to stay in bed with this traction thing for several weeks; then they'll take me back to surgery to fix it permanently, and then start teaching me to walk on crutches. Oh, great! Several weeks!

So that explains how I got here, and this account I'm writing now is part of my school work for English. Maybe it will help me find out if I really can be a writer. I can't think of anything else to say now so I'll just continue it every day and tell about what has happened to me that day.

Sunday night

Well, it's late, almost midnight. I've had company all day. Sunday must be the day everybody comes to visit sick people.

I was glad to see a lot of the kids in my class, but they sure were loud. I was so tired after a while that I just wished everyone would go home, or at least be quiet.

I think the nurses were a little mad because the guys were talking loud and acting silly and the girls were squealing and giggling and some of the kids tried to sit on my bed. Bouncing the bed hurt, and bumping my leg *really* hurt. I tried to tell them that, but they just ignored it. And with all the crowd, the nurses were having trouble getting in and out so they could give me my medicine and take care of my roommate.

Hospital food isn't very good, so a bunch of the kids went out and brought in hamburgers and pizza. It tasted great, but boy, what a mess when everyone left. There was stuff piled up everywhere that the nurse had to clean up. I could tell she wasn't happy with me, and I was embarrassed for myself and embarrassed for my friends, acting like that.

Well, things weren't going that great, but when some of the kids who had had to work that evening tried to sneak in after visiting hours, the nurse got really mad. She didn't say very much, but she didn't *have* to say very much! I've got to set some of the guys straight.

I was so beat I went right to sleep and forgot to do this writing assignment. Now I'm awake again, and I decided to do it before trying to go back to sleep.

Monday morning

One thing is for sure, everything starts early in a hospital. They woke me up before 7 a.m. to check my temperature, blood pressure, and heart. I told them it was too early, that my heart hadn't got started yet, but they did it anyway.

Next came the breakfast trays. I haven't mentioned it, but it's pretty weird lying flat on your back and trying to eat. I usually manage to spill something, and it usually goes down my neck. But I'm getting better at it.

My bed has buttons to push that can raise the head of the bed a little to make things easier. I can't raise it very much, because that messes up the angle of the traction on my leg.

Once breakfast is over, the next delight of my day is a bed bath. If I thought eating meals in bed was weird, it's nothing to compare with having a nursing assistant give me a bath in bed. They set a plastic pan of water on the bedside tray and let me wash off with a washcloth as far as I can reach; then they finish washing the parts of me that I can't get to because I can't sit up.

Next they change the sheets on my bed—with me in

it. This involves several nurses coming in and just lifting me a few inches to pull out the dirty sheet and push a clean one under me, and then pulling it tight and tucking it in place.

It's really strange. I thought nurses just took your pulse and gave shots and things like that. But they have to do stuff I never even thought of. But I guess it's nothing new to them.

Today was kind of a bummer. It probably sounds silly, but it's the first time the whole thing has seemed *real*. I mean, the first few days I was sort of out of it, and then the weekend was busy and I had a lot of visitors and everything, but today it's quiet and I think about people going back to work and back to school and it has really hit me, like, wow, I'm stuck! I'm going to be in this place for *weeks*.

I guess I was snappish and crabby to the nurses, because one of them sat down and talked to me for a little while. She said she understood how I felt, because everyone felt the same way at first, but don't take it out on the people around me.

Felt like a worm after that. I mean, these nurses work their buns off, and I'm acting like that. I swear I do not intend to do it again!

Tuesday afternoon

It's after lunch now and there's not much on TV except soap operas. Ugh! Wish I could go to a movie or just get out of bed to do anything at all. Lying still like this is boring. It's deadly. My back hurts from lying on it like this. I even wish I was back in school. Now I *know* I'm sick!

My leg has been hurting a lot today, and I had to ask for some pain medicine. It was a shot. I've had to have quite a few shots, and they switch between putting them in my arms and in the thigh of my left leg. They try not to put them in the same places to keep them from getting sore, but everyplace is getting sore now.

After the shots I get real sleepy, and sometimes I sleep through meals. The nurse today told me they would change me to pills so I could be awake more. I'm afraid of shots, but I wonder if the pills will keep my leg from hurting.

Wednesday night

My parents brought me some books and magazines today and some posters for my wall. There's not much room, but it's nice to have something to look at and it makes it more like home.

I've had three different roommates since I've been here, and tonight the other bed is empty. They were all in for minor things and usually were up running around. I didn't see much of them, so it's been almost like being by myself.

Some of the guys came by after school today, and I was glad to see them. Guess I've really been missing out on a lot at school right now. They said one of the teachers was going to come up tomorrow and bring me assignments and homework and everything.

I've been here one week now and it sure seems like a long time. I didn't know how much difference a week would make, but they brought me pictures of Rod's car, and seeing it I just started to shake. One of the guys got so uptight he called a nurse!

I can tell you, I feel pretty lucky right now!

Rod came up tonight just before visiting hours were over. (They took him to a different hospital after the wreck.) He acted kind of like he was afraid I would blame him. I told him of course I didn't blame him. I saw the light and that it was green as clearly as he did. It wasn't our fault the trucker was asleep at the wheel or whatever was wrong with him.

Rod's face is all cut and scratched and scraped, and we can't figure out how that could have happened. But it did.

Forgot to mention—I have gotten a lot of nice flowers and tons of get-well cards. And everybody who could get hold of a cartoon of a patient with his leg in traction has sent me one! Never would have thought there could be so many. But it's kind of nice, too.

Very late Wednesday night

Hospitals are spooky at night. I woke up and the TV was off—I mean the channels were off, and there was only something on the one that stays on all night. I thought of calling the nurse and asking for a sleeping pill, but I didn't. I just lay there and thought how different it all was—all the lights dim, and the place quiet—and I started thinking about other people who are here. People with things that aren't like broken bones that you know will get all right.

For some reason I got to thinking about a girl in my sixth grade class, who had leukemia. Funny—I hadn't thought of her in years. I didn't know her well or anything; she'd just started in my school that year. She was there a few weeks and then gone and then back again, and then we heard she was in a hospital. She died that summer and we'd hardly seen her, she'd hardly been to school at all.

Funny to be thinking about that. I felt on edge, tense, like I was waiting for something to snap, break, I don't know. There was something like electricity in the air.

Then, just as I was making myself relax, the PA system came on and said, "Code Blue. Code Blue Six East." The PA system hardly ever comes on at night, and it really startled me. But the next second the hall was full of people running and equipment carts and things.

I could see the guy in the room across the hall come to the door, holding his "air conditioned special" around him, trying to see what was going on.

Everyone went into a room at the end of the hall, and even thought they were quiet about it, you knew it was something bad.

It seemed like a long time, and then I heard them moving something big down the hall. It clinked and rattled and seemed to be moving fast, and when they passed my door I could see a lot of people in white moving a whole bed, with IV bottles and stuff. They weren't running, but they were moving pretty fast.

I couldn't see the person in the bed, just that whoever it was had dark hair. You could tell by the way the people looked that whatever had happened wasn't good.

I lay here a long time thinking about that, and about myself, and what I'm going to do in life and everything. I feel different about things. Maybe being in here has made me grow up a little. Be more mature.

Didn't think I'd get back to sleep, but I'm starting to nod off now. Can just see the first hint of daylight outside.

Thursday morning

I'm getting used to the pin through my leg now, and

moving doesn't seem to bother me as much now. I'm also getting used to the baths and changing of the sheets, but there's one thing I'll never get used to.

I thought eating in bed and taking a bath in bed were pretty weird, but they're nothing compared to using a—you guessed it!—bedpan.

I guess this isn't a great subject for a school assignment, but it's part of being in the hospital so I'll mention it without going into gruesome details.

All of us take very much for granted being able to walk into a bathroom and do what we have to do in private. Well, I've found there's very little privacy and not too much modesty left when you can't get out of bed. So when it gets to be the time of day when nature calls, I have to call for help. The nursing assistant brings me a plastic, oblong flat pan known—not very affectionately—as a bedpan, and then the ordeal proceeds.

I'll leave it to the imagination how it all works, but it does work, and I'll simply say it is not fun.

Friday night

Today has been long and kind of scary. Late last night they brought in a new roommate. I don't think I should use names here, so I'll call him Mr. X.

I guess he got sick and had to come to the hospital, because he had had an operation on his stomach. He was put in my room after the operation, and his wife was sitting with him. He had tubes from his nose that went to a machine that made sucking noises all night pulling liquid out of his stomach. The nurses kept coming in every few minutes to check on him, taking his blood pressure, and then I think he started getting worse.

They gave him a lot of medicine and several doctors came in to see him, and then they rolled him out to take him back to surgery. His wife was crying and I felt bad, but I didn't know what to say or do.

I don't know what happened to him, but he didn't come back here. I felt bad that I didn't try to talk to his wife. I really felt like a kid—I mean six years old with my thumb in my mouth—lying here watching them and not having any idea what to do or say. I guess that's what they mean, getting hit with the real world.

I've been awfully surprised at one thing about being in the hospital—it affects your mind, not just your body. I won't be the same person when I go home.

The nurses laugh and tease me a lot, but they sure do seem to know when something is wrong. They knew I was on edge about Mr. X today, and that helped me handle it.

Sunday night

Well, I had so much company yesterday that I didn't write anything, and almost as many kids came to see me today. I'm tired but wide awake now, even though it's after 11.

Just saying what I do everyday seems boring, because I do the same things over and over, so I'll write about the nurses. They work three shifts. Day shift is from 7 a.m. to 3:30 p.m., evening shift is from 3 p.m. to 11:30 p.m., and night shift is from 11 p.m. to 7:30 a.m.

The day nurses seem rushed and have a lot to do, giving baths and medicines and sending patients to X-ray and surgery and other places. That's when the doctors make their rounds to see their patients, too.

I've discovered that the doctor has to write down

everything that I'm allowed to do, from medicine to what kind of food I get to eat. I can't have even so much as an aspirin for a headache unless he orders it. I guess the doctors are like principals in school. Their word is law around here.

I'm getting tired now, so I'll continue with what the other shifts do later.

Monday afternoon

Really getting tired of this bed. I never knew how nice it is just to be able to get up and walk around. The pin through my leg is bothering me today. It looks like a big nail with silver tongs attached to each end where it comes out on either side. The tongs are tied to ropes that go over the end of the bed on pulleys and are fastened to weights that bang and move around when I move in bed or when somebody accidentally bumps them.

Three times a day the nurse cleans the areas of skin where the pins are and puts medicine on them to keep them from getting infected. At first I wouldn't even look at them, but it doesn't bother me now.

Well, let me get back to what the evening shift nurses do. They care for people back from surgery and other places, which takes a lot of time, because patients coming back from surgery aren't very awake so they have to be checked a lot.

There are usually a lot more visitors in the evening, especially on weekdays, and I guess that keeps the nurses busy, too. They give all the medicines, sleeping pills and things, and straighten out the beds so people can get comfortable and sleep. I guess they miss a lot of television, too. I wouldn't want to work evenings.

The night nurses check on all the patients while they

sleep and give all the medicine and whatever else needs to be done.

They used to wake me up coming in the room, and I asked why they did it all the time. They explained that a lot of the patients are really sick and need to be checked on frequently to see if they need anything.

I think they mean they need to make sure nobody dies while asleep, because they shine flashlights on patients to see if they are still breathing. It must be sort of creepy. I wonder if they feel like burglars, walking so softly and looking all around a room with just a flashlight.

They go home and sleep in the daytime, which must be weird, but I guess they like it.

Tuesday night

Well, I got the big news today that I'm going to surgery in the morning to get the pin in my leg taken out and have a cast put on. I'm sure glad, because then in a few days I'll get out of bed. My doctor said I'm doing so well he's able to take out the pin a lot sooner than he thought.

It's almost 11 p.m., and I can't have any food or water after midnight because I might get sick to my stomach while they are giving me the anesthesia in surgery, and if I vomit it might go into my lungs.

Yuck!

They said that could be dangerous, so I guess I'll just go thirsty. That's better than getting sick.

I'm kind of nervous about tomorrow, but it sure will feel good to get out of bed.

Thursday morning

Yayyy!! I'm actually sitting up in bed this morning and will get out of bed this afternoon! I'm a few pounds heavier now with the cast on my leg. It goes all the way up my thigh and is just now getting dry. It was wet when they put it on, and the plastic dries slowly.

The physical therapy department is going to teach me how to walk with crutches this afternoon, and then I can get up and around and maybe go home in a few more days.

Thursday night

Well, I'm mobile again. In a manner of speaking. It was like learning to walk all over again. Crutches aren't as easy to use as they look like they'd be. For one thing, you can't lean on them with the tops in your armpits. That can cause serious damage to the nerve that runs down into your arm. So you direct the real strength down your arms into the hand grips. The physical therapist said it would build up my arm muscles and to think of it as pumping iron!

I sure never thought I'd be so dizzy and weak from being in bed just a few days. My muscles feel like rubber. I was sort of dizzy and kept wobbling around trying to get used to standing up and handling the weight of the cast. But I'm practicing again this evening and getting better at it.

Some guy from the next room came out in the hall and started to tell me what I was doing wrong and how to walk with crutches and everything—just snapping orders at me. I felt like whacking him with a crutch, but figured it would make me fall down.

I told a nurse, back in my room, what a geek I thought he was. She didn't say anything, but she looked like she thought so, too.

Friday night

Well, this is the final entry!

I'm at home!

I ran around so well on the crutches that they let me out. Now I know what a paroled prisoner must feel like.

The hospital really wasn't that bad, and I learned a lot, especially about myself.

But it sure feels good to be home!

Index